MVFOL

RALPH S. MOUSE

What They're Saying About RALPH!

SCHOOL LIBRARY JOURNAL BEST BOOK

"Full of amusing vignettes
and sudden insights."
—*The Horn Book*

"Children will eagerly read
these further adventures of Ralph."
—*School Library Journal* (STARRED REVIEW)

NO TIME TO TALK

"Look, Ryan," he said. "I'm in trouble, and I don't have time to tell you about it. Just take me and my motorcycle with you, and don't ask questions."

"To school?" Ryan was surprised.

"Come on," begged Ralph. "We're friends, aren't we?"

"Sure we're friends," agreed Ryan, "but—"

"There's no time for buts," said Ralph, who knew Ryan would soon have to leave to catch the school bus.

"Well, OK, if you say so," said Ryan.

By the time "OK" had passed Ryan's lips, Ralph was wheeling out his motorcycle with his crash helmet dangling from the handlebars.

BEVERLY CLEARY

RALPH S. MOUSE

ILLUSTRATED BY
JACQUELINE ROGERS

SCHOLASTIC INC.

ISBN 978-0-545-79446-6

12 11 10 9 8 7 6 5 4 3 2 1   14 15 16 17 18 19/0

Printed in the U.S.A.   40

This edition first printing, September 2014

Typography by Sarah Nichole Kaufman

CONTENTS

1

A DARK AND
SNOWY NIGHT

Night winds, moaning around corners and whistling through cracks, dashed snow against the windows of the Mountain View Inn. Inside, a fire crackled in the stone fireplace. The grandfather clock, as old and tired as the inn itself, marked the passing of time with a slow *tick . . . tock . . .* that seemed to say, "Wait . . . ing, wait . . . ing."

Everyone in the lobby was waiting—the desk clerk, the handyman, old Matt, who also carried guests' luggage to their rooms, Ryan Bramble, the son of the hotel's new housekeeper, and Ralph, the mouse who lived under the grandfather clock.

The desk clerk dozed, waiting for guests

who did not arrive. Matt leaned against the wall to watch television while he waited for the desk clerk to close up for the night. Ryan, sitting on the floor to watch television, waited for his mother to tell him to go to bed because he had to go to school the next day. Ralph, crouched beside Ryan, waited for the adults to leave so he could bring out his mouse-sized motorcycle. Unfortunately, Ralph's little brothers, sisters, and cousins, hiding in the woodpile and behind the curtains, were also waiting.

On the television set, a sports car crashed into a truck, shot off a cliff, and burst into flames.

"Wow!" Without taking his eyes from the screen, Ryan said, "There's a boy at school named Brad Kirby, who would really like this movie. He has a BMX bicycle for motocross racing, and his father sometimes drives him to school in a tow truck." A police car followed the sports car over the cliff before Ryan added, "Brad isn't very friendly to me. He's sort of a loner."

Ralph was more interested in television than in Ryan's problems. "If I had a sports car like that," he said, "I wouldn't let it run off a cliff."

Ralph was an unusual mouse. He had listened to so many children and watched so much television that he had learned to talk. Not everyone could understand him. Those who could were lonely children who shared Ralph's interest in fast cars and motorcycles and who took the trouble to listen. Other children, if they happened to glimpse Ralph, said, "I saw a mouse that squeaked funny."

Matt was the only adult who understood Ralph. "Yes, sir, that mouse is a mouse in a million," he often told himself.

Ralph knew there were not really a million mice in the inn, although he had to admit that in wintertime the mouseholes were crowded, because his rough outdoor relatives moved inside to keep warm. Ralph's mother said they were a rowdy bunch that set a bad example for the more civilized indoor mice.

While Ralph and Ryan were enjoying a commercial for a truck that could zigzag without overturning, Matt strolled into a room called the Jumping Frog Lounge and returned with a handful of popcorn. He dropped one kernel in front of Ralph.

"Thanks," said Ralph, who enjoyed nibbling popcorn while watching television.

As the commercial ended, Mrs. Bramble entered the lobby. "Come on, my boy," she said to Ryan. "It's past your bedtime. You know the manager doesn't like you hanging around the lobby."

"Aw, Mom, just let me watch the end of the program," pleaded Ryan. "I'll leave if any guests arrive."

At that moment, the rattle and crunch of a car with chains on its tires was heard. Ryan rose and walked backward out of the lobby so he wouldn't miss the high-speed, siren-screaming chase on the television screen. As he left, he gave Ralph a little wave with his fingertips, a wave no one else would notice. Ralph wished Ryan could stay up all night like a mouse.

As the car stopped in front of the hotel and the desk clerk roused himself, Ralph scurried under the grandfather clock to the nest he had made from chewed-up Kleenex, a lost ski-lift ticket, and a few bits of carpet fringe he had nipped off when no one was looking. Beside his nest rested his two precious possessions: a little red motorcycle and a crash helmet made from half a Ping-Pong ball lined with thistledown, gifts of a boy who had once stayed in the hotel.

Above Ralph the clock began to grind

and groan and strike, *bong . . . bong*, as if it had to summon strength for each stroke. Ralph dreaded the sound, even though it was the reason he lived under the clock. The noise terrified his little relatives, who thought the clock was out to get them. As long as they feared the clock, Ralph's motorcycle was safe.

The car door slammed. Feet stomped on the porch. When Matt opened the door to let two people blow into the lobby, a blast of freezing air sent Ralph's nest swirling around in bits. Never mind, thought Ralph, peeking out at two pairs of boots, the kind known as waffle stompers, which had thick treads that held snow.

"Do you have a room for the night?" the owner of the larger boots asked the desk clerk.

"H-mm, let's see," murmured the clerk, who always behaved as if the hotel might be

7

full even though he knew it was not.

Stop pretending, thought Ralph, who was tired of waiting.

"Well. . ." The desk clerk ended the suspense. "I can let you have Room 207. Just fill out this card, please."

Ralph's keen ears heard the scratch of a pen and the rattle of a key. He winced when the clerk banged the bell on the desk for Matt, even though Matt was standing right there, waiting to carry the guests' bags.

"Never mind," said one of the guests to Matt. "We can find our room." The pair picked up their luggage and stepped into the elevator, leaving behind puddles of melted snow.

"Cheapskates," muttered Matt. Guests at this hotel often insisted on carrying luggage to avoid tipping him.

After the elevator door closed, Ralph worried that the puddles might dry before he had the lobby to himself. Time dragged on. The man in the red vest who worked in the Jumping Frog Lounge came out, yawned, and remarked that he might as well close for the night. The television station went off the air. The desk clerk locked the front door and left. If any more guests arrived, they would have to ring the night bell. Matt began to turn out the lights.

At last! Ralph threw his leg over his motorcycle, adjusted the rubber band that held his crash helmet in place, and grasped his tail so that it would not become tangled in his spokes. Then, because as everyone knows, a toy motorcycle moves when someone makes a noise like a motorcycle, Ralph took a deep breath, went *pb-b-b, b-b-b*, and shot out from under the clock. Gradually he picked up speed and zoomed through a puddle. Wings of water fanned out from his wheels. It was a thrilling experience.

All of Ralph's little brothers, sisters, and cousins, hoping Matt would not notice them in the dim light, popped out from their hiding places to watch. Of course, Ralph had to show off. He took deeper breaths and rode faster, making puddles splash higher and leaving tiny tire tracks on the dry linoleum. Matt, who was banking the fire for the night,

laid down the poker to enjoy the sight.

Unfortunately, the little relatives were not satisfied. Not now. Once Ralph's indoor relatives had been happy to have Ralph push them up and down the halls on his motorcycle, but this treat was not enough for his rowdy outdoor relatives. They wanted to ride the motorcycle by themselves, so now all the mice wanted to ride. They came running and jumping, across the threadbare carpet, to the linoleum, squealing, "I want a ride!" "Gimme a turn!" "Come on, Ralph, get off and let us use it!"

Ralph started to whiz around in a figure eight when his tires slipped and the motorcycle tipped. He lost control and landed in icy, dirty water.

The daring outdoor mice waded out to grab the motorcycle, but Ralph was quick. Dripping and shivering, he sprang back on the seat and rode off, *pb-b-b, pb-b-b*, avoiding clutching paws. If only he could make his relatives behave. "Go away. You're too little," said Ralph through chattering teeth, as he swerved to miss tiny toes. "You would forget to hang on to your tails, and you'd get them tangled in my spokes." He tried to wipe his nose with his wet paw and wished mouse children had to go to bed at night like human children.

"We would not!" The rougher mice grabbed the motorcycle and brought Ralph to a halt. "And you're not so big yourself. You fell down."

All the mice began to complain. "You let us ride, or we'll tell your mother on you. She said you were supposed to give us a turn." Cousins closest to Ralph in age said it wasn't fair for Ralph to have a motorcycle. Nobody had ever given them motorcycles, and they were just as good as Ralph. Some of the meaner mice told him their mothers said Ralph was spoiled and selfish and would probably turn out to be no good when he grew up.

Ralph was hurt. "I am not spoiled, and I am not selfish," he insisted, as he tried to drag his motorcycle away from all those

clutching paws. In his heart, he did not feel selfish. He only wanted something that was his alone. A mouse so rarely had something he could call his own.

"You're greedy," said a cheeky outdoor mouse. Then all the mice, down to the littlest one who was tangled in the fringe of the carpet, began to chant, "Ralph is greedy, Ralph is greedy!"

Ralph finally lost his temper and squeaked at the top of his voice, "Beat it, you rotten little rodents!"

"Try and make us." The outdoor mice were defiant, but Ralph could tell they were not as brave as they pretended.

Shocked and hurt by such strong language, the little indoor mice fell silent. They looked at Ralph with such sad eyes that Ralph was ashamed. "You said bad words," said one, his voice filled with reproach.

"I'm going to tell on you," said another.

"My mother wouldn't like you to call me— those words."

Ralph felt terrible. "Aw, come on," he said. "It's just that my motorcycle is wearing out. The tires are thin, and if they wear out, where am I going to get another pair?"

The little mice would not accept this excuse. "We've never had a motorcycle at all," one of them said.

"I know, but—" began Ralph, not knowing how to finish. It was not his fault his young relatives did not have motorcycles. Still, maybe he had used language too strong for little ears. He was only trying to make his pack of pushing, shoving, grabbing relatives behave.

Matt must have understood Ralph's feelings, for he came to his rescue. "Shoo!" he said loud enough to frighten little mice but not loud enough to terrify them. The word sent them scrabbling back to their hiding places.

"Thanks," said Ralph.

"Think nothing of it." Matt gave the fire one last poke before he retired for the night. He left the rapidly drying puddles for Ralph, who took another turn through them. Although water still fanned out from his wheels, somehow the fun had gone out of riding for that night.

Wearily Ralph pushed his motorcycle back to the cave under the clock where it was safe. Even though he was wet and numb with cold, he lovingly wiped mud and paw prints from his chrome spokes with bits of shredded Kleenex. When he began to wipe his exhaust pipes, he discovered they wiggled, loosened by all those tugging paws. The rear wheel shock absorber was loose too.

When Ralph had wiped off all the mud and had polished his chrome, he rummaged through the remains of his nest for a bit of carpet fringe. Unfortunately, it turned out to be too thick for tying his exhaust pipes in place. He felt worse and worse as he began to groom his damp fur. His tires were so thin he no longer wanted to risk the wear of riding them on the rough surface of the carpet. His motorcycle was wearing out. None of his relatives liked him. They were going to tattle on him. In the morning, his mother would venture downstairs to lecture him on the evils of selfishness and bad language. She would also lecture him on his duty to set a good example for little mice.

Ralph pushed his nest together again. I'm a bad mouse, he thought, filled with gloom and guilt. *I* am a rotten rodent, not my relatives. As he climbed into his nest and curled up with his tail tight around his body, he wished he could leave the Mountain View Inn so he would never have to face them again. But how could a mouse leave in winter

when there was snow on the ground and
wind howled? He would freeze, starve, or
be blown away. Or all three. Ralph shiv-
ered and pulled his tail more tightly around
his body.

2

RALPH'S DECISION

After his strenuous night of riding through puddles, fending off his relatives, trying to repair his motorcycle, and rebuilding his nest, Ralph napped soundly. He was awakened by the angry voice of Mr. Minch, the hotel manager, speaking to Mrs. Bramble, Ryan's mother.

"Look at that floor," Mr. Minch was saying. "Disgraceful!"

"It certainly needs a good cleaning," agreed Mrs. Bramble.

"Where's Matt?" demanded Mr. Minch. "Keeping this lobby clean is his responsibility."

Worried because his friend was in trouble, Ralph peeped out from under the clock and saw Matt, unaware of the manager's displeasure, enter the lobby. "Morning, Mrs. Bramble, Mr. Minch," Matt said. "It's sure pretty outside with the sun shining on the snow and the sky so blue."

Mr. Minch ignored this greeting. "Matt," he said, and his voice was stern, "take a good look at this floor. Dried mud on the linoleum. Mouse droppings all over the place. It's a disgrace. And the whole lobby smells—well, mousey."

That's funny, thought Ralph. I can't smell a thing.

Matt looked at the floor. "Well, I'll be

jiggered," he said. "How do you suppose that happened? It looked clean enough last night."

Liar, thought Ralph with affection. He knew Matt would never say a bad word against mice.

"Never mind how it happened," said Mr. Minch. "Exactly what do you plan to do about it?"

"Now take it easy, Mr. Minch," said Matt. "I'll have this place cleaned up in no time."

"See that you do," said Mr. Minch. "This may not be a first-class hotel, but there is no excuse for a dirty lobby. I realize that late arrivals often leave muddy floors, but mouse droppings—! If I continue to find signs of mice, I shall have to let you go."

That's not fair, thought Ralph, who did not want to lose his loyal friend. Matt had been part of the hotel as long as he could remember, much longer than either Mr. Minch or Ryan's mother. Most employees did not stay long at the Mountain View Inn.

"Yes, sir." The cheer had gone out of Matt's voice.

Ralph, who came from a long line of intelligent mice, knew that most of his relatives had learned to avoid traps and poisons. He was not so sure about his littlest relatives, however. What was left after traps and poisons? Cats. Ralph shuddered at the thought of bloodthirsty cats stalking his innocent little brothers, sisters, and cousins. The littlest one, who always became entangled in the carpet fringe, would be the first to go.

A skier who was looking at headlines on the newspapers on the rack near the door overheard the conversation between Matt and Mr. Minch. "There's a new electronic mouser on the market," he volunteered. "It makes a noise only mice can hear and drives them out of the building in a hurry."

"I'll look into it. Something has to be

done around here," said Mr. Minch, as he returned to his office.

Ralph shuddered at the thought of an electronic mouser sending his family screaming into the snow to freeze to death.

Mrs. Bramble wanted to say something pleasant to Matt after the unhappy incident. "One good thing about the ski crowd," she remarked, "they may track in snow, but they don't bother to drip-dry a lot of clothes and clutter up the bathrooms." With that cheerful remark, she went upstairs to count sheets and towels in the linen room.

"More like a fourth-rate hotel, if you ask me," muttered Matt, who had seen better days. He dragged out the vacuum cleaner. "Old Minch will never spend a nickel on an electronic mouser. How am I supposed to get rid of mice? Say, 'Please, mousies, go away so old Mr. High-and-mighty won't throw me out in the cold'?"

As the vacuum cleaner roared back and forth across the carpet, Matt looked so worried that Ralph began to worry too. What if the old man really did lose his job in the middle of winter? Where would he go? And what would Ralph do without his friend? He noticed that in spite of his worries, Matt did not run the vacuum cleaner near the hems of the curtains, a favorite hiding place of mice.

Ralph sat back on his haunches and began his morning grooming. As he wiped his paws over his whiskers, he suddenly had a most unhappy thought. He was to blame for Matt's trouble. If he had been an ordinary mouse without a motorcycle, all his little relatives would not have come flocking into the lobby. They would still live upstairs, snug in their nests behind the baseboards, growing fat on crumbs from all the food skiers smuggled into their rooms to avoid the dining-room prices.

Ralph paused in his washing to think. If he moved back upstairs, his relatives would follow. But what about his motorcycle? He couldn't leap up a flight of stairs with it; neither could he leave it behind. Never! If he left it behind, some of his older cousins would grab it and stay in the lobby—at least until they wore it out or wrecked it—and the younger relatives would stay too.

What was Ralph to do? He was still turning over this problem in his mind when the clock above him ground and groaned and managed to bring out eight bongs. Right on schedule, Ryan came running into the lobby, warmly dressed to go to that mysterious place known as school. He was carrying his books and lunch in a backpack. Ralph admired his waffle stompers.

The muddy floor caught Ryan's attention. He studied the mud, and when Matt left to fetch a mop, he got down on the floor in front of the clock and pressed his cheek against the floor so that he could speak to Ralph. "I saw your tire tracks," he whispered. "I bet you had a great time last night."

"Yeah, except for a bunch of little mice," said Ralph.

"What's the matter?" Ryan asked him. "You sound unhappy."

Suddenly Ralph knew what he had to do. He thought fast, which was easy for him. Mice often have to think fast to survive. "Look, Ryan," he said. "I'm in trouble, and I don't have time to tell you about it. Just take me and my motorcycle with you, and don't ask questions."

"To school?" Ryan was surprised.

"Come on," begged Ralph. "We're friends, aren't we?"

"Sure we're friends," agreed Ryan, "but—"

"There's no time for buts," said Ralph,

who knew Ryan would soon have to leave to catch the school bus.

"Well, OK, if you say so," said Ryan.

By the time "OK" had passed Ryan's lips, Ralph was wheeling out his motorcycle with his crash helmet dangling from the handlebars. "I'll stay out of sight," he assured his friend. "There must be someplace I can live at school."

Ryan stuffed the motorcycle into one pocket of his parka and picked Ralph up carefully so he wouldn't smash his tiny ribs. "You mean you want to *stay* at school?"

"Yes," said Ralph, suddenly frightened by his decision. "There must be someplace I can hide."

Ryan thought a moment. "Well, there's one of Melissa Hopper's boots. You could hide there."

"Doesn't she wear her boots?" asked Ralph, picturing himself squashed in the toe of a boot by the foot of Melissa, whoever she was.

"Not if she can help it," said Ryan. "Melissa hates boots, so she leaves them at school. That way her mother can't make her wear them."

A sensible girl, thought Ralph.

Mrs. Bramble came bustling back into the lobby. "Ryan, what on earth are you doing on your knees? You should be on your way out to the highway, or you'll miss your bus."

"Just checking the floor for dust," fibbed Ryan, as he quickly slid Ralph into his parka pocket. "Bye, Mom." And he ran out the door and went crunching through the snow to the highway.

Ryan must have had second thoughts about taking Ralph to school. He said, "I guess Miss K won't mind."

"Who's Miss K?" asked Ralph.

"My teacher," explained Ryan. "Her real name is Miss Kuckenbacker, but she told us to call her Miss K, because calling her Miss Kuckenbacker would take up too much classroom time."

"Oh," said Ralph, mystified.

To Ralph, school was a strange and mysterious place. When he had been a very young mouse, Ralph had pictured school as something like a bus, because mothers and fathers who arrived at the hotel with several children after a long, hot drive across the Sacramento Valley or the long, winding ride over the Sierra Nevada often said, "I'll be so glad when school starts." Ralph had naturally concluded that because a school started, it must also move like a car.

As Ralph had grown more sophisticated from listening to children, he came to understand that children moved. Schools stood still. Later on he learned that some grown-ups called "teachers" also went to school. Some of these teachers stayed in the hotel during the summer. As far as Ralph could see, teachers behaved like ordinary people except that, unlike parents, they said, "Oh, dear, school will soon be starting."

Ralph found a clue as to what teachers did in that mysterious place from a television commercial shown several times a day. In it, a woman who said she was a teacher held a tube of toothpaste in her hand as she walked around saying, "Toothpaste doesn't excite me. Good checkups excite me."

This remark puzzled Ralph, however. When he had lived upstairs, he had once tasted toothpaste when a careless guest left the cap off a tube. He found himself foaming and frothing at the mouth as he skittered around frantically trying to find water while one of the maids ran down the hall shrieking, "Mad mouse! Mad mouse!" No, Ralph could not agree with the television teacher. Toothpaste *was* exciting.

"This Miss K," said Ralph, as Ryan reached the bus stop. "Is she OK?"

"Yeah, she's pretty good." Ryan stamped his feet to keep them warm. "She thinks up interesting things to do for language arts. Like our school is named the Irwin J. Sneed Elementary School, and last week she had us write a composition about who we thought Irwin J. Sneed was and why the town of Cucaracha, California, named its school after him." Ryan scooped up a handful of snow, squeezed it into a ball, and threw it at the branch of a pine tree. Snow slid off the branch and fell with a soft *plop*.

"Some kids made Irwin J. Sneed a monster from outer space," continued Ryan, "but I made him a horse thief back in the gold-rush days when Cucaracha was a mining town. I said he was the first person to go to jail in Cucaracha, so they named the school after him. Miss K gets real excited about Cucaracha being a gold-rush town with a lot of history."

"Oh," said Ralph, puzzled. "Who was Irwin J. Sneed really?"

"Just some old guy on the school board when the school was built way back in the 1970s," explained Ryan, as he made another snowball.

Ralph could make no sense of this information at all.

As the snowball made more snow plop from a branch to the ground, Ryan had a sudden thought. "I better be careful about talking to you at school, or people will think I'm nuts."

"Maybe some of them could understand me," suggested Ralph. "They might even like to see me ride my motorcycle."

Ryan considered. "You better not go

showing off. Somebody might steal your motorcycle, or maybe everybody would start bringing mice and motorcycles to school. I don't think that would be a good idea, a whole school full of mice tearing around on motorcycles. One mouse can get by, but not a lot of mice. You know how some people get all worked up about mice."

As the school bus came rumbling down the highway, Ralph had to agree from his hotel experience that Ryan was right. One mouse, or even two or three, could get by. Many mice could not. "Say," he said, "you don't suppose there are already mice in this place."

"No," said Ryan, as the bus stopped in front of him. "Mr. Costa keeps our school too clean for mice."

Of course, Ralph's feelings were hurt.

"Remember to keep out of sight," were Ryan's last words to Ralph as he climbed on the bus.

Deep inside the parka pocket, Ralph felt sad, brave and noble, frightened and bewildered. He felt sad because there had been no time to say good-bye to Matt. He felt brave and noble because his going out into the strange world would protect the safety of his little relatives. He felt frightened and bewildered because so much had happened so fast. Yet the inside of the pocket was cozy. In the deepest corner, Ralph found a dried-up raisin that would have made an excellent breakfast if he had not been so nervous about what lay ahead in that mysterious place, the Irwin J. Sneed Elementary School. He nipped a tiny bite of the raisin and told himself school must be safe because so many children went there. Of course, I will be all right, he told himself, pretending to be brave, but I will be careful to stay away from Miss K's toothpaste.

3

IRWIN J. SNEED ELEMENTARY SCHOOL

As Ryan hopped down the steps of the school bus, Ralph poked his nose out of his pocket and found himself in a crowd of children, all of them bundled up in hooded parkas or jackets and knit caps. Clouds of vapor came from their mouths as they shouted back and forth to one another. A tiny cloud formed in front of Ralph's nose, too.

A boy jumped out of a yellow tow truck and shouted, "So long, Dad!" Then, as the truck pulled away, he added, "So long, Arfy," to the dog sitting next to the driver.

"Arf," answered the dog, who looked like a kindly wolf.

That boy must be Brad, thought Ralph, as the children trampled snow on the playground on their way into the long one-story building that was the Irwin J. Sneed Elementary School.

Inside the building, the linoleum-floored hall, unlike the halls of the Mountain View Inn, was a broad smooth highway with no rough carpets to wear down the already thin tires of a little motorcycle. Ralph wondered how he could endure a whole day of waiting for night to come so he could race down that long hall. There would be no furniture to get in his way and no little relatives to make him feel guilty for not sharing his motorcycle. That hall was the perfect race-course Ralph had dreamed about ever since he had owned a motorcycle. With no one around to see him take spills, he could even rear back on one wheel to practice wheelies.

Ryan entered Room 5, a room different from any room Ralph had ever seen. Unlike the rooms at the inn, this one was furnished with many chairs and tables instead of beds. At the front, seated at a desk, was a woman Ralph knew must be Miss K. Her toothpaste was nowhere in sight.

At the rear of the room, Ryan hung his backpack on a hook. Then he removed his parka and hung it on the hook, too.

"Hey, don't leave me here all by myself," squeaked Ralph, alarmed at being alone in such a strange place. "Take me with you."

"Promise you'll stay out of sight?" whispered Ryan out of the corner of his mouth.

"Sure," agreed Ralph.

Ryan started to poke Ralph into the pocket of his jeans until Ralph objected. "Hey! Not here. This place is too tight. You'll squash me when you sit down."

"Sorry," said Ryan, and he dropped Ralph into the breast pocket of his plaid flannel shirt.

No sooner had Ryan sat down at the table than he and the rest of Room 5 stood up again to recite some words about a flag and something about liberty and justice for all. Whatever it was, Ralph hoped mice were included.

Ryan sat down and began to shuffle books and papers while Miss K talked about numbers. Ralph tried to listen above the steady *lub-dub*, *lub-dub* of Ryan's heart, but soon he grew bored. Ryan's shirt was new and the flannel still fuzzy. Ralph nipped a hole in the front of the pocket for a better view and then, lulled by the muffled *lub-dub, lub-dub* and the steady rise and fall of Ryan's chest, fell asleep as if he were being rocked in a cradle. Because a heart does not strike the hours like a clock, Ralph slept until recess and again until lunchtime when Ryan remembered to slip a bit of sandwich into the pocket for his lunch.

Sometime in the afternoon Ralph awoke feeling hot, cramped, and restless. Maybe no one would notice if a small brown mouse poked his nose out for a breath of air. After a few whiffs, Ralph stuck his head all the way out to see what was going on. All heads, except one, were bent over papers on the tables. One girl was chewing her pencil and staring into space.

That's funny, thought Ralph. I didn't know people gnawed things too.

Unexpectedly, the girl turned her head and looked straight at Ralph. Then she tapped another girl on the shoulder and pointed.

Too late, Ralph ducked back into the pocket. He heard the girls whispering, and soon others were whispering too. Oh, oh, thought Ralph, feeling both guilty and doomed. He had broken his promise to stay out of sight. He was in trouble.

Miss K spoke. "Melissa, is something disturbing you?" she asked.

Melissa, thought Ralph. So that's the girl

whose boot I'm supposed to live in.

"Not exactly, Miss K," answered Melissa.

"There seems to be something going on that I don't know about," persisted Miss K. "Won't someone let me in on it?"

"I—uh—thought I saw something move in Ryan's pocket," admitted Melissa.

"Ryan, do you have something you wish to share with the class?" asked Miss K.

Ralph squeezed himself into a corner of the pocket as Ryan's heart began to beat faster, or rev up, as Ralph thought of it.

"No, not exactly," Ryan told his teacher.

The class began to speak. "Yes, he does." "He does too." "I saw something and it moved."

Ralph dug his claws into the flannel shirt as Miss K said, "Ryan, why don't you come to the front of the room and let us see what it is?"

Ralph started to chew through the side of the pocket closest to the heartbeat.

As Ryan walked to the front of the room, he reached into his pocket, grasped Ralph by the tail, and dragged him, clawing and struggling, out of the pocket. Ralph was so angry at this treatment he was squeakless. When Ryan set him on the palm of his hand, he turned his back to the class and sat quivering with rage and terror.

"What a beautiful mouse!" said Miss K, who was young and enthusiastic and eager to give her pupils learning experiences. "Class, gather around for a better look."

I'm beautiful? thought Ralph. No adult, or child for that matter, had ever described him as beautiful. Far from it.

"Look at his perfect little paws," said Miss K.

Ralph looked too as the class left their seats to crowd around. His paws looked like ordinary mouse paws to him, but now that she mentioned it, maybe . . .

"And his lovely little ears," continued Miss K.

"Aw—" breathed the children. "He's cute." "He's really neat." "He's darling!"

Well, what do you know? Ralph perked up and stopped quaking. Shyly he turned to face the class.

One member of Room 5, however, did

not admire Ralph. "He's just your standard brown mouse," said Brad. "There are plenty more like him."

"Where did you get your mouse, Ryan?" asked Miss K.

"At the hotel where I live," explained Ryan. "He's a very smart mouse. His name is Ralph."

"What's his last name?" someone asked.

"Mouse," answered Ryan. "His name is Ralph S. Mouse. The *S* stands for Smart."

"May I hold Ralph?" asked Miss K, and Ralph found himself transferred to a softer, cleaner hand. He sat up and began to groom his whiskers, always a good performance. He could see that Ryan was happy to be receiving so much attention from his classmates.

"Aw—" breathed the class again. "Look at him. He washes like a little cat."

"Such a tiny scrap of life," said Miss K. "He's a little miracle."

Ralph stopped wiping his paws over his whiskers to look with love at Ryan's teacher. Her long shiny hair fell over her shoulders. It looked so strong that Ralph was sure that just one of her hairs would be perfect for tying his exhaust pipes in place.

"Perhaps the custodian has a cage we could keep him in," said Miss K.

Love turned to distrust. This wonderful woman with useful hair was turning out to be like any other grown-up.

Ryan spoke up. "I don't think Ralph would be happy in a cage," he told his teacher. "I'll just keep him in my pocket if it's all right with you." Good old Ryan.

Miss K gently handed Ralph back to Ryan, who stuffed him into his shirt pocket. "Thank you for sharing Ralph," she said above the *lub-dub* of Ryan's heart, now steady as a well-oiled motor. "Class, how would you like to draw pictures and write stories and poems about mice? Friday afternoon we could have a mouse exhibit to show off our work. Ryan, you could bring Ralph to school again so he could be our guest of honor." Miss K, who had no idea Ralph was planning to live at school, was a teacher who could turn anything into a project.

Most of the class was enthusiastic. Others thought mice were as good a subject as any for drawing and writing. A boy named Gordon said he didn't like to do any of those things. Miss K suggested he could go to the library, look up facts about mice, and write an essay about them. "And what do you want to do, Ryan?" she asked.

"I would like to tell how smart Ralph is." Ryan's answer threw Ralph into a fright. What was Ryan going to tell his classmates about the motorcycle? Ralph would *not* ride his precious motorcycle in front of everyone.

"Splendid, Ryan," said Miss K, "but why not show us how smart he is? Do you know what a maze is?"

"Sort of," said Ryan. "I've seen them on the kid's page of the Sunday paper. You take a pencil and try to draw a line through the open spaces of a diagram from one side to the other. It isn't easy, because there are a lot of dead ends."

"That's right," said Miss K, who was drawing a maze on the blackboard as Ryan spoke. "Scientists use mazes with walls to test the speed with which mice learn. They start a mouse at one end and time him to see how fast he reaches food at the other end. Then they have him do it again. If he cuts down his time, they know he has learned from the experience. Do you think you could build a maze?"

"I'd like to try," Ryan answered.

"Good," said Miss K. "I'll bring a stop watch for timing Ralph's race through the maze."

"I can bring my cap pistol for a starter's gun," volunteered Brad, showing interest for the first time.

"Good idea," said Miss K. "You like to build things, so perhaps you could help Ryan build his maze."

The boys eyed one another as if they

were not sure how a partnership would work out. "Uh—OK," agreed Brad.

So it happened that Ralph was not only a learning experience for Room 5, he was to have a learning experience of his own. He was not sure he liked the idea, especially that part about the starter's gun. What if he couldn't run through the maze faster the second time? What if he couldn't find the food the first time? What if he turned out to be stupid?

Of course, I'm not stupid, thought Ralph, as he tried to make himself comfortable in Ryan's pocket once more. I can ride a motorcycle, can't I? He began to have doubts again, and doubt turned to anger. His intelligence or stupidity was nobody's business but his own.

When the last bell rang and Ryan went to the back of the room to collect his parka, Ralph poked his nose out of the shirt pocket.

"I'm not going to do it," he squeaked at Ryan. "I'm not going to run any maze just because you say so."

"Sure you are," said Ryan out of the corner of his mouth, so no one would notice he was talking to Ralph. "I'm new in this school, and nobody paid any attention to me until I pulled you out of my pocket. You have to run the maze."

Ralph became stubborn. "No, I don't," he contradicted, "and you can't make me."

Ryan ignored this remark. "Do you want to change your mind about staying here? You can go back to the inn with me."

"I'll stay here," answered Ralph, thinking of that long smooth hall waiting for his motorcycle. "I can't let Matt lose his job."

Ryan looked around to make sure no one was watching before lifting Ralph out of his pocket and placing him in an overturned boot. "So long. See you tomorrow," he said.

"Who're you talking to?" a boy asked.

"Me?" Ryan was all innocence. "Nobody. I'm just practicing to be a ventriloquist. I'm working up an act—"

"Some act," remarked the boy.

Ryan held up one hand and waggled his fingers as if he were working a puppet's mouth. "What did one dandelion say to the other dandelion?" he asked in a squeaky voice without moving his lips. "I don't know," he said in a normal voice. Then he answered in his squeaky voice, "Take me to your weeder."

All this nonsense made Ralph frantic. "Hey, gimme my motorcycle!" he ordered, as soon as the other boy had gone.

Ryan tried to speak without moving his lips. "And have you riding all over school? Not a chance. You'd get lost or get into trouble or someone would see you."

"It's my motorcycle," squeaked Ralph at the top of his lungs. "You give it to me. *Now*."

Ryan was last to leave the room. "We'll see about that," he said, as he bent over to speak to Ralph, "after you run the maze on Friday." With that ultimatum, he snatched his backpack off the hook and hurried away to catch the bus that would take him back up the mountain to the hotel.

Ralph was so angry he sank his teeth into Melissa's boot. Ugh. It had a nasty taste— half rubber, half dust. And he had thought Ryan was his friend. Not anymore. He was mean, he wasn't fair. . . .

Ralph felt terrible, but he was *not* going to run that maze in front of Room 5. Ryan couldn't make him. Maybe he would even hide and refuse to be guest of honor. Ryan would learn not to try to order him around then.

Ralph sat in Melissa's boot and sulked.

Without his motorcycle, he felt mad at the whole world. Of course, he was a smart mouse. Why should he have to prove it? Ralph felt as if nothing was fair and nobody loved him.

4

LIFE AT SCHOOL

Dusk began to fall in Room 5, making the inside of Melissa's boot even darker, when suddenly Ralph heard music, the lights were turned on, and a man with a transistor radio fastened to his belt came into the room and lifted chairs onto tables. He began to sweep with a wide broom while the radio poured forth sad songs about lonely highways, broken hearts, and jail.

The songs made Ralph feel gloomy as well as sulky. He began to feel sorry for himself—the long hall so perfect for motorcycle riding was dark and empty, his heart was broken over the loss of his motorcycle, and he might as well be in jail as in this old boot.

When the man swept his way to the back of the room, he unexpectedly set Melissa's boots upright side by side, tumbling Ralph down to the foot, where he sat trembling with nerves and self-pity until his ears told him the man had replaced the chairs on the floor, turned off the lights, and left.

Because he was a mouse, Ralph found sleeping at night almost impossible. Without the grandfather clock to mark the hours, the night seemed endless. Why should I sit here in this smelly old jail of a boot when everyone is so mean to me? Ralph asked himself. And with the cruelty of the world as an excuse for breaking his promise to Ryan, he used his sharp claws to climb the boot lining. Quickly he leaped out and squeezed under the door of Room 5. Nobody was going to stop him from exploring the Irwin J. Sneed Elementary School.

After a long and wistful look at the lonely highway of the hall, Ralph found exploration more interesting and profitable than he had expected. In Room 4, he discovered strange-looking pictures spread out on the floor beneath the blackboard. They were made by gluing different kinds of seeds to heavy paper and had been left on the floor to dry. Ralph made a nutritious meal of split peas, rice, and lentils before moving on to another room where he found an open jar of library paste—delicious! Another room, furnished with long tables and benches, was near a kitchen, where Ralph chewed into a bag of sugar and enjoyed a fine dessert.

After this gourmet meal, Ralph walked rather than scampered down the hall, that perfect place for riding his motorcycle if Ryan had not been so mean, to a room with a carpet and bookshelves about the walls.

A boring place for a mouse, Ralph decided, until he discovered something interesting on a bottom shelf behind a big desk. It turned out to be a book inside a bag made of two layers of brown paper. A tear in the outer layer revealed something unexpected in the lining.

Ralph could not believe the treasure he had found. Between the layers of paper was ready-chewed mouse nest! Ralph pulled out some of the nest to examine its delicate texture—first quality, grade-A mouse nest. He made the hole in the bag still larger, crawled inside, and curled up in the coziest bed he had ever known.

Ralph intended to rest there while he plotted to get his motorcycle away from Ryan, but his full meal made him drowsy, and instead he fell asleep. Awaking to the sound of school buses, he ran back to Room 5 just in time as his former friend was hanging up his parka.

Ralph ran up the leg of Ryan's jeans and onto his shirt. "You gimme my motorcycle," he demanded, trying to sound fierce.

Ryan quickly faced the corner so no one could see Ralph. "Be quiet. You're not supposed to be here," he whispered. "Like I said, I'll give it to you after you run the maze."

"Who says I'm going to run it?" Ralph was sullen about this whole affair.

"I do." Ryan tried to speak without moving his lips. "If you want your motorcycle back."

"Where is it?" Ralph wanted to know.

"Right here." Ryan removed the motorcycle from his parka and placed it in one of his shirt pockets. "Now go back to your boot."

"Don't call it my boot," said Ralph. "It's dusty and smelly."

"Will you be quiet if I let you stay in my pocket?"

"Sure." A shirt was warm and soft and had a good view of the classroom if a hole was nipped in the pocket.

As he dropped Ralph into his pocket, Ryan said, "And another thing. Don't chew any more holes in my pockets. Mom didn't like it when she saw holes in the new shirt I wore yesterday."

We'll see about that, thought Ralph, determined not to let the *lub-dub* of Ryan's heart lull him to sleep again until he figured out how to get that motorcycle back. For a better view of Room 5, he bit a careful peephole—one thread down and one thread across—in Ryan's pocket.

Ralph watched with puzzled interest while the class worked with numbers and words. Late in the morning the children formed a double line, something Ralph had never before witnessed, and walked quietly to the library, where they selected books to read. Why can't mice behave like that? Ralph wondered.

When Ryan had found the book he wanted, he took the little red motorcycle out of his pocket and amused himself by running it back and forth across a table while softly going, "*Pb-b-b-*." The sound was enough to break a mouse's heart.

The most interesting part of the day turned out to be late in the afternoon when the class worked on their projects for what the children called the Great Mouse Exhibit. Miss K read a poem that Ralph found difficult to understand, something about a "wee, sleekit, cow'rin, tim'rous beastie" while the class worked with crayons and paper. Ralph saw strange pictures of himself beginning to emerge. They were making him look very *big* except for one boy who drew a cat that filled up the whole paper and then added a tiny mouse down in one corner.

Other boys and girls bent over their

paper, writing, pausing to gnaw their pencils, writing again. Others behaved strangely, nodding their heads, tapping their pencils, and softly chanting ta-*dum*, ta-*dum*, ta-*dum* or ta-ta-*dum*, ta-ta-*dum*. The noises sounded something like an Indian war dance in an old movie on TV, thought Ralph, puzzled.

Ryan and Brad worked with glue and some old cartons on a table at the back of the room. They moved around so much and Ralph's peephole was so small he could not get a very clear idea of what they were building. Apparently they did not have a very clear idea themselves, for they argued about the way to make the partitions of the maze stand up, about the height of the partitions ("We don't want him to be able to see over them, even if he stands on his hind legs"), and the length and number of the blind alleys. Mostly they argued about the difficulty of the maze.

"Let's make it really hard," said Brad.

Ralph decided he did not like Brad with his tousled hair, grubby T-shirt, and unfriendly ways.

"Not too hard," said Ryan.

"Aw, come on," said Brad. "Making tunnels and trapdoors would be fun."

"Real mazes aren't like that, and it wouldn't be fair," protested Ryan. "He's just a little mouse. Besides, we haven't figured out how to make the partitions stand up."

"You're scared he can't do it," said Brad.

"Of course, he can do it." Ryan was at least loyal.

But what if I can't do it? Ralph worried. What if I run around bumping my nose against dead ends? Then how would Ryan feel after all his bragging? A terrible thought occurred to Ralph. If he failed and everyone laughed, Ryan might not give back the motorcycle after all.

Ralph decided there was only one thing
to do—get up on that table at night and
practice. He would memorize the maze so
he could dash through the passages without
bumping his nose even once.

Ralph had no sooner made this decision than part of the maze must have fallen down, for Ryan said, "See, I told you it wouldn't work that way."

Brad lost patience. "All right," he said, "since you're so smart, you can make your own dumb maze for your own dumb mouse. I'll write a poem instead."

"You don't like to write poems," Ryan reminded him.

"I'd rather write a poem than work on your dumb maze for your dumb mouse," answered Brad. "His name should be Ralph D. Mouse. *D* for Dumb."

"OK," said Ryan. "Suit yourself, but I don't see why you have to be so touchy all the time."

Good, thought Ralph. Ryan will make it easy.

When the last bell rang, Ryan asked permission to work on the maze at home because he still hadn't figured out how to make the partitions stand up.

"Of course, you may," Miss K told him, thereby destroying Ralph's plan to practice. "I hoped you and Brad might become friends if you worked together." She raised her voice above the scramble for jackets and caps. "Class, I have a surprise," she announced. "Someone who writes stories for the *Cucaracha Voice* heard about our mouse exhibit and wants to write it up for the paper. She is going to come Friday afternoon and bring a photographer." Cucaracha, although it had grown since gold-rush days, was still a small town. News traveled fast.

There was a buzz of excitement. Room 5 was going to have its picture in the newspaper!

When Ryan plucked Ralph from his pocket, Ralph asked in his tiniest voice,

"Do I get a chance to practice running through that thing before Friday?"

"That would be cheating," said Ryan through stiff lips. "The same as looking at test questions before a test."

"Just one little peek?" coaxed Ralph.

"Nope." Ryan poked Ralph into Melissa's boot and ran off to catch his bus.

Ralph crawled down around the bend to the toe of the boot, where he sat brooding in the dusty, musty dark. For the first time since he had left the inn, he began to wonder if anyone missed him in his old home.

5

THE GREAT
MOUSE EXHIBIT

Ralph spent the rest of the week dread-
ing Friday. The days, in spite of all that
went on in Room 5, dragged, but the nights
passed more quickly. As soon as the man
with the transistor radio and broom left
Room 5, Ralph squeezed under the door
and ran into the next classroom. The pictures made of seeds were now hanging
above the blackboard, but enough split peas

and lentils had fallen to the floor to make a good meal for Ralph. In the kindergarten room, he discovered a doll's house, which he enjoyed exploring. Still, even though it had a mouse-sized bed, it lacked the comfort of the ready-chewed mouse nest in the library.

One night, however, Ralph had a narrow escape. Beside the book bag on the library shelf, he discovered an interesting contraption, something like a metal snail. Of course, Ralph had to investigate and found his back stuck to something he had not known about—Scotch tape. The rest of the night was spent trying to free himself. When he had almost pulled his back free, his paws were stuck. When his front paws were unstuck, the strange sticky tape trapped his back paws and tail. Exhausted, Ralph managed to free himself as the first bus rolled up to the school.

Wednesday morning Ryan informed

Ralph he could not sleep in his pocket any longer, because Ryan's mother said his shirts smelled funny. Once again Ralph's feelings were hurt. Ryan also said his mother had discovered the tiny peephole Ralph had nipped in his shirt.

"She would," said Ralph.

Ryan defended his mother. "Maybe she's fussy, but she's a good housekeeper. That's why the hotel hired her, which was lucky for us. She really needed the job."

Probably all mothers found something to fuss about, Ralph decided, even though his own mother was a poor housekeeper. He wished Melissa were fussier as he retired to the dark and dirty tunnel of her left boot. He missed the lulling *lub-dub* but found staying awake in class and paying attention to Miss K much easier. The next day someone dropped a woolly mitten, and it made a restful change from the boot.

Thursday afternoon Miss K said, "Ryan, don't forget to bring our guest of honor tomorrow."

"I won't forget," promised Ryan, as if he did not know Ralph was lurking at the back of the room.

The next morning, after his usual night of enjoying all that the school had to offer a lonely mouse, Ralph stayed awake to groom himself because he wanted to look his best when he was the honored guest. The members of Room 5 also wanted to look their best for their picture in the newspaper, and they came to school looking neater than usual. Even Brad was wearing a clean T-shirt. Ryan brought the finished maze to school and placed it on the table at the back of the room far above Ralph's head.

Drat, thought Ralph, and he ran up Ryan's leg in hopes of a glimpse of the test that lay ahead. Ryan quickly popped Ralph into his pocket before he had a chance to look.

Just before the last period, when the Great Mouse Exhibit was about to take place, Ryan pulled Ralph out and took him to Miss K. "Welcome, Ralph," she said. To Ryan, she said, "Put our little guest of honor in the fishbowl on my desk. Then everyone can see him."

To Ralph's horror, he found himself placed in a slippery glass bowl. Frantically

he scrabbled about, trying to find a way out. When he found there was no way to escape and no place to hide, he sat quaking with indignation, a wee, sleekit, cow'rin, tim'rous beastie, just as the poem said.

As the bell for the last period rang, the guests arrived. They were Mr. Tanner, the principal; Mrs. Seeger, the librarian; Mr. Costa, the custodian; and Room 5's room mother, who brought twenty-six little bags of popcorn for a treat. The Great Mouse Exhibit was about to begin.

"Where're the reporter and photographer?" someone asked.

"I'm sure they'll be along soon," answered Miss K, and she welcomed the visitors. Then she introduced the guest of honor, who turned his back and tried to become invisible. She pointed out all the pictures of Ralph above the blackboard. As if I looked like *those*, thought Ralph with a sneer.

Then Miss K said some members of the class had stories and poems about mice they wanted to share with their guests. She called on Brad, who slouched to the front of the room, announced that he wasn't much good at poems, and that his poem was sort of dumb. He read:

"Ralph is a mouse.
He's stupid, he's dumb.
He's as bad as a louse.
He belongs in a slum."

With a triumphant look at Ryan, Brad slouched back to his seat.

"Thank you, Brad," said Miss K, who seemed uncertain as to an appropriate comment. "That was—very amusing."

Ralph thought of several impolite things she could have said as he walked nervously around his prison, wondering how much longer before he would have to run that maze. He sniffed to test his sense of smell. Enclosed in glass, all he could smell was himself.

A girl named Janet was next. "My poem is a limerick," she told the audience and read:

> "A mouse once came to our school
> And quickly broke every rule.
> He got stuck in our paste
> For he liked its good taste,
> So he said, 'I'll just sit here and drool.'"

The audience laughed, and Janet, flushed with pleasure at her success, returned to her seat.

That's a lie. I didn't go near Room 5's paste, thought Ralph, as he trotted nervously around the fishbowl to make sure his legs worked.

Gordon, the boy who did not like to write stories and poems, was next, but before he could begin his essay, the door opened and a young woman entered, followed by a man hung with cameras. "Sorry to be so late. We had to cover a big story about a truckload of chickens loose on the highway." The reporter from the *Cucaracha Voice* was out of breath. "Now go ahead with your program, and pretend we aren't here."

Flustered by the photographer prowling around adjusting his lens, Gordon began to read, "Mice are rodents. They gnaw things and they multiply rapidly."

They do not, thought Ralph. He had watched Miss K multiply by writing squiggles with chalk on the blackboard. He had never seen a mouse do any such thing. The photographer was now circling the fishbowl with the black eye of the camera aimed at Ralph. *Click. Click. Click.*

I hope he isn't around when I have to run that maze, thought Ralph, darting around the fishbowl, trying to avoid that evil eye.

Gordon read on, the reporter scribbled,

the photographer turned toward the audience, the class sat up straight and smiled. "Mice are harmful," Gordon read. "They destroy crops and food supplies. They kill trees by gnawing around the bark. Mice can be destroyed by traps, poison, and cats."

That's *mean*, thought indignant Ralph. We aren't harmful on purpose. We're just trying to get along in a harsh world.

Gordon continued. "It has been said that if you see one mouse, there are twenty-five mice hiding that you don't see."

Ralph thought this statement over. It might be true of the inn, but it was not true at Sneed Elementary.

The class was silent. Mrs. Seeger looked pleased, for she had helped Gordon find information about mice. The reporter thanked Miss K for letting her visit—good story—great angle—sorry she couldn't stay—mayor cutting ribbon for opening of new auto-parts shop—meeting of the school board. With that apology, she dashed out the door, followed by the photographer weighed down with cameras.

Ralph tried to keep his legs flexible by running short sprints around the fishbowl. He must not let his muscles tighten before the race.

Melissa was next. She paused to smile at Ralph before she announced, "The title of my story is 'The Strange Disappearance of Ralph.'"

Ralph stopped sprinting to listen.

Melissa read, "A mouse named Ralph lived at the house of a girl named Primrose. Primrose liked Ralph. She let him run all around the house. One day Ralph was in the laundry room. Primrose's mother told her to take the clothes out of the dryer. Primrose did not see Ralph. Some of the clothes she pulled out of the dryer fell on top of Ralph. A nylon sock with static cling stuck to Ralph. When Primrose folded all the clothes, she had one sock left over. The sock with Ralph stuck to it was gone. It had gone wherever socks with static cling go when they get lost. The sock and Ralph were never seen again. The end."

The class thought the story was funny. Ralph did not know what to think. He had learned about static cling from watching those boring women who talked about it on television, but could he really stick to a sock? What a terrible thought. Just to be safe, he had better stay away from socks from now on.

Melissa was happy with the success of her story until several members of the class asked why the girl's mother had not used Static-off in her wash.

"She just didn't," answered Melissa. "I guess she didn't watch TV."

"I am not so sure a sock would really cling to a mouse," said Gordon, a thoughtful boy always interested in facts.

Oh, shut up, thought Ralph. These delays were making him nervous. A ray of winter sunshine fell on the fishbowl, making it so warm that Ralph began to pant.

Gordon's remark did not bother Melissa. "The sock clung to him in my story," she said, as if her answer ended the discussion.

"But the sock had to be someplace," persisted Gordon.

The class took up valuable time defending Melissa's story. Oh, no, socks didn't have to be someplace. Socks disappeared at their houses all the time. They could look every place and never find them. Nobody knew where they went. Sometimes they couldn't find matching socks to wear to school. Their mothers had drawers full of socks without mates. Gordon did not know what he was talking about. One girl said her mother took the family's washing to the Laundromat and often came home with socks she had never seen before.

Why didn't they all shut up and let him run? Ralph began to worry lest Miss K think up a project to find out if a sock with static cling would adhere to a mouse. The discussion came to an end when Mrs. Seeger offered to look up information on static electricity for the class.

Gloria was next. "My poem is called a haiku," she announced. "It is a kind of poem the Japanese write. It never rhymes, but it always has seventeen syllables." Gloria paused a moment until she had the complete attention of the class before she read:

"A little brown mouse
Smells cheese and steps in a trap.
Snap! Now he is dead."

Ralph was so horrified that he curled up in a tight ball to stop his trembling. How was he supposed to run a race if he was shaking all over? The class, preferring verse that rhymed at the end of lines, was silent, not knowing what to think of Gloria's poem.

"I think that was mean," volunteered Melissa.

"Well, I think it was good." Gloria was defiant.

Cruel, thought Ralph. Cruel and murderous.

"An excellent haiku, Gloria," said tactful Miss K, "but let's hope such a thing never happens to Ralph."

Mrs. Seeger said she would look up haikus for Room 5, and Miss K said she would read them aloud.

"We haven't much time left," said Miss K, "and now our guest of honor will demonstrate how quickly he can learn."

Ralph had waited so long to run that excitement had drained out of him, leaving him heavy with dread. Ready or not, he must begin his trial. His motorcycle depended on it, even though his legs were stiff and his entire body trembled.

6

THE MAZE

"Come on, Ralph, old buddy." Ryan scooped Ralph out of the fishbowl. "Show them how smart you are." No one thought there was anything unusual about Ryan speaking to Ralph when Ralph was in plain sight. Children often talked to their pets.

Ralph struggled in Ryan's hand, which smelled of the egg sandwich he had eaten for lunch.

"Take it easy, Ralph," said Ryan. "You can do it."

"I need to warm up first," squeaked Ralph.

Ryan paid no attention. Possibly he did not hear because of the murmurs of excitement as pupils gathered around for a better view of the maze. He set Ralph down in front of an opening in a cardboard wall and said, "When Brad fires his cap pistol, go for the peanut butter."

Ralph shook his paws in a last desperate attempt to limber them. At the same time he sniffed, trying to get wind of the peanut butter at the end of the maze. Unfortunately, the room was full of confusing odors—popcorn, tomato sauce of tacos eaten by those who bought school lunches, peanut butter, bologna, egg, orange, banana eaten by those who brought lunches from home. Ralph caught a whiff of grape bubble gum, the reek of sweaty socks, and the scented-soap fragrance of Miss K.

By the time the teacher said, "On your mark," Ralph was completely muddled. He crouched, waiting for the starting gun, which did not go off.

"My caps are stuck," said Brad.

After the heat of the fishbowl, the cooler air made Ralph's muscles feel rigid. He felt as if he had been waiting forever.

At last Brad fired his cap gun. *Bang!*

"Go, Ralph, go!" shouted the class.

The noise was enough to unnerve the bravest mouse. However, since Ralph was pointed toward the opening of the maze, he knew where to start. He ran through the opening and bumped his nose against a cardboard wall. Then he turned the other way.

"No!" shrieked the children. "Not that way! The other way!"

Ralph followed their direction and bumped his nose again. My motorcycle, he thought in despair, I'll never get my motorcycle back if I don't do it right.

"Ralph! Don't let me down." Ryan's voice rose above the shouting.

Down among the partitions of the maze, with so many lunch-smelling rooters breathing on him, Ralph had no idea of the direction of the peanut butter.

"Ralph D. Mouse!" Brad yelled.

"Everybody shut up and give him a chance!" screamed Melissa.

Suddenly Ralph was angry. He knew he was really a smart mouse. Why should he have to run around banging his nose in front of all these tacos and sandwich gobblers? Nimbly he leaped to the top of the partitions, caught a whiff of pure peanut butter, and took off across the top edges of the maze. He would show them who was smart.

Ralph was halfway to the peanut butter when he felt Ryan's egg-sandwich smelling hand close around his body. "Hey," said Ryan, "you aren't supposed to do it that way."

Ralph, feeling that the world was unfair, found himself back at the beginning of the maze. He was furious. No one had said he had to bump his nose on every single dead end in the maze. Why should he? The

object was to reach the peanut butter as fast
as possible.

"On your mark," said Miss K a second
time.

Bang went the cap gun.

Ralph leaped to the top of the partition,

nimbly raced across the top of the maze, and filled his mouth with peanut butter just as the last bell rang and the room mother began to pass out bags of popcorn.

Ryan picked up Ralph and poked him into his shirt pocket. "I *told* you that wasn't the way you were supposed to do it." He sounded disgusted.

Ralph, who was unable to defend himself when his jaws were stuck with peanut butter, felt Ryan was most unjust.

"Class, I wish we had more time," said Miss K, as her pupils crunched popcorn and scrambled for their wraps. Time and school buses waited for no one.

"Hey, Melissa," said Ryan, "how come you're taking your boots home?"

"Because my mother says I can't watch TV all weekend if I don't," answered Melissa.

Ralph struggled to free his jaws. Would

he get his motorcycle back, or wouldn't he? He had to know.

"Ralph Dumb Mouse," said Brad.

"Just because you don't have a mouse." Ryan sounded angry as he slid his arms into his parka. "You're jealous. That's what you are."

"Who wants a smelly old mouse?" scoffed Brad. "You stink, and so does Ralph D. Mouse."

"You shut up," said Ryan.

"Make me," said Brad.

Ralph was terrified by the sound of scuffling. With great effort, he freed his jaws and managed a muffled squeak. "Me! I'm here in your pocket! Don't let him hit me!" His voice was so smothered by the parka that no one could hear him, but Ryan must have remembered. He cupped one hand over his pocket, which left only the other hand for protecting himself. He was pushed, bumped against someone, and fell to the floor.

The class began to shout, "Fight! Fight!" and crowd around as popcorn scattered.

"Boys!" Miss K's usually gentle voice cut through the commotion. "Hurting people does not solve anything. It only makes things worse."

Ryan got to his feet. Ralph, shaken but relieved to find himself uninjured, peeped out of the shirt pocket. To his horror, he saw Ryan reach into the pocket of his parka and pull out a crushed crash helmet and a little red motorcycle broken in two.

His precious motorcycle, his only means of transportation—four feet didn't count—was destroyed. Ralph experienced the darkest moment of his life.

"I'll get you for this, Brad," said Ryan, as Ralph slid back to the depths of the pocket. "You broke Ralph's motorcycle."

Brad laughed. He could. He had not

been knocked down. "Are you crazy or something?" he asked. "What do you mean, Ralph's motorcycle?"

"Boys, that's enough," said Miss K. "Hurry

along, Ryan, or you'll miss your bus."

In the hall, Ralph emerged from the pocket to confront Ryan. "Now see what you've done because you wouldn't give me back my motorcycle. You've gone and wrecked it."

Ryan, flushed and humiliated, turned on his friend. "I don't care if your motorcycle is broken," he informed Ralph. "It serves you right for not doing what you were supposed to. I never should have brought you to school in the first place. See what happened because I tried to be Mr. Nice Guy."

"Some nice guy," said Ralph with a tiny snarl. "Wouldn't even let me have my own motorcycle, and now look at it. Busted. Well, I've had enough, I'm getting out of here." With that declaration, Ralph climbed out of Ryan's pocket, ran down his jeans, and jumped to the floor, dodging waffle stompers and boots as he fled.

"Hey, watch it," called Ryan. "Don't get stepped on." He turned and ran for his bus.

Ralph dodged feet until he was safe against the wall, where no one would step on him or even notice him in the crowd. As soon as all the children had left, he made his way to the library without bothering to nibble any of the popcorn squashed on the floor. The torn book bag in which he had enjoyed such comfortable naps was gone, but he found a fresh bag, gnawed a hole in the brown paper, and crawled into the soft, ready-chewed stuffing. How good it felt—warm, cozy, and comforting—after all he had been through this terrible afternoon.

In the hall, Mr. Costa was sweeping up popcorn with his broad broom while his transistor radio sang a sorrowful song about a broken-hearted man trying to hitch a ride on a lonely stretch of highway while the coyotes howled in the night.

After Mr. Costa left, the school was a silent, deserted place. The next morning the children did not return. Ralph, who did not understand that there was no school on Saturday and Sunday, had never been so alone in his life. He stood in the cold and empty hall and squeaked as loud as he could, but his tiny voice could not even raise an echo. All weekend he roamed the desolate halls and classroom, halfheartedly nibbling whatever he could find to eat, going *pb-b-b* because he missed his motorcycle so much, and wondering if he was doomed to roam forever the lonely corridors of the Irwin J. Sneed Elementary School. Why didn't the children return?

Ralph thought of the old hotel with its shabby lobby warmed by a crackling fire. He missed the reassuring tick of the rasping old clock. He missed watching television and the activity in the lobby—the arrival and departure of guests and the arguments among the staff. He missed old Matt, his protector, and supplies of peanuts and popcorn from the Jumping Frog Lounge. He wondered if his plan to make the little mice leave the lobby had worked and if Matt still had his job.

Ralph discovered he even missed—sort of—his little brothers and sisters and cousins. He wondered if the littlest one still fell over his own feet and became tangled in the fringe of the carpet. He wondered what they would say if they could see him now, cold and lonely, in the vast empty school. He also wondered what they would say if he went home with Ryan without his motorcycle. Something like, "Yah, yah! Serves you right for not wanting to give us rides."

The scoffing of his relatives was something Ralph could not face. Never. As he walked slowly back to the book bag in

the library, he heard a dog bark in the dis-
tance and was reminded of the coyotes that
howled in the night in the song about the
lonely man trying to hitch a ride on the
highway. What a sad world he lived in.

7

THE CUCARACHA VOICE

Sometime late Sunday night the weather changed. Snow began to melt. By Monday morning, the fleet of school buses came sloshing through slush. Boots and waffle stompers tracked mud and icy water into the halls of Irwin J. Sneed Elementary School, where the wearers were met by Mr. Costa holding a large mop.

Ralph, whose weekend had been so long

and so lonely, felt such a surge of joy and relief at the sound of school buses that he skittered back to Room 5 in a forgiving mood. There he hid in the old mitten. Anything, *anything* was better than that long, cold, miserable weekend, and perhaps Ryan had found a way of repairing the motorcycle.

Miss K's class arrived in a grouchy mood. Snow was fun; slush was not. There was more confusion than usual as the children peeled off their wraps and kicked off their boots. Many were carrying clippings from the *Cucaracha Voice*. Miss K was not in the room to welcome them, which did not help.

Gordon told Melissa, who was wearing wet shoes and carrying her boots, that he was sure static electricity would not hold a mouse to a sock. Melissa told Gordon he had no imagination.

Brad arrived with his arm in a sling. Instantly a rumor started that Brad had hit Ryan so hard he had injured his hand. Sides were taken; arguments began.

Ryan glared at Brad. "You owe me a motorcycle for the one you broke. Serves you right if you hurt your hand."

"That motorcycle you said was Ralph's," scoffed Brad. "What would that stupid mouse do with a motorcycle?"

Someone dropped a clipping, and before it was picked up, Ralph was able to glimpse a picture of himself looking small and frightened in the goldfish bowl. The picture was not bad; in fact, it was quite good. His eyes were bright, and each hair was distinct. Ralph congratulated himself on being such a handsome mouse and wondered if Matt back at the inn—if he still worked there—would see the picture, recognize, and perhaps miss him.

As the last bell rang, Miss K hurried into the room with a worried look on her face. Instantly she was surrounded by excited children, waving clippings from the *Cucaracha Voice* and trying to talk at once. "It wasn't like that at all!" they said. "That reporter got it all wrong!" "It's a bunch of lies!" "They didn't even put our picture in the paper." Most puzzling was, "Ralph isn't that kind of mouse. He's nice!"

They're behaving like a bunch of little mice, thought Ralph. At the same time, he wondered uneasily what the paper had said about him. That he wasn't nice? Impossible.

Miss K stood without speaking at the front of the room. Gradually the class grew quiet. "That's better," said Miss K.

Amazing, thought Ralph. The teacher had silenced the class without using a single bad word. He was even more ashamed of the way he had treated his little relatives.

After the class recited liberty-and-justice-for-all (But not for me, thought Ralph), Miss K said, "Class, we have a lot to talk about this morning, and we can't talk if we all speak at once. Brad, suppose you begin by telling us what happened to your arm."

Brad looked embarrassed. "Aw, I just sprained it when I tried to ride my bike in the mud. I was trying to get ready for the first motocross race this spring."

The class respected what Brad had tried to do, and Ralph was struck by a sudden thought: Brad was exactly the sort of boy who could understand a mouse who rode a motorcycle.

To change the subject, Brad asked, "Is Ralph going to try to run the maze again?"

"How about it, Ryan?" asked Miss K. "Did you bring Ralph to school today?"

"He's lost." Ryan sounded worried. "He got mad because . . . Well, he got mad

Friday afternoon and disappeared."

"I am not lost," Ralph said to himself. "I know where I am, right here in this mitten."

A sigh of disappointment ran through Room 5. The class liked Ralph. Besides, watching a mouse in a maze was more fun than social studies or spelling.

"Miss K," said Gordon, "even if Ryan finds Ralph, I don't think he should have to run the maze again. He proved there was a better way to get the peanut butter than running into dead ends."

Why, he's right, thought Ralph, perked up by Gordon's support. I'm smarter than I thought I was.

"Class, do you agree?" asked Miss K, who liked her pupils to think.

The class thought. Brad was first to speak. "In motocross racing, it's against the rules to get off your bike. I think he cheated."

Several people were quick to point out

that testing intelligence with a maze was not the same thing as racing on a bicycle, even a BMX.

"Maybe he was too a-mazed to do it right," suggested Melissa with a giggle.

"Well, I think he proved he was Gifted and Talented." Gloria spoke as if she had ended the discussion by using words the school used to describe children such as herself.

Miss K asked for a show of hands. Twenty-one children agreed that Ralph had found a better way to run the maze. Five felt he cheated. Case settled. Ralph was an unusually smart mouse, something he had doubted only once in a while.

"Speaking of solving problems," said Miss K, "do you think fighting is a good way to settle arguments?"

"No!" chorused the girls.

Ryan defended himself. "Brad pushed me

first. Besides, it wasn't a fair fight, because I had Ralph in my pocket and didn't want him to get hurt."

"What do you have to say, Brad?" Miss K asked.

"He made me mad, always bragging about how smart his mouse is and then trying to make the maze easy." Brad slid down in his chair. "Anyhow, how was I supposed to know he had his old mouse in his pocket?"

Ryan muttered to Brad, "Just because you get to come to school in a tow truck you think you're so big."

"Just because you get to live in a hotel you think you're better than anybody," mumbled Brad.

These remarks were lost to the class because the girls, bored with the scuffle discussion, were waving their clippings from the *Cucaracha Voice*. "Miss K," said Gloria, "I think that reporter was unfair. What she said about us was all wrong."

Some members of the class, protesting that their families did not subscribe to the *Voice*, demanded to know what the article said.

Miss K read the headline aloud. *Class Nabs Sneed Invader.*

What's she talking about? wondered Ralph, moving from the mitten to Melissa's overturned boot for a better view. What invader?

Miss K continued. "Under Ralph's picture, the story reads, 'Friday afternoon the fifth-grade class of Miss Bambi Kuckenbacker at Irwin J. Sneed Elementary School exhibited a mouse, thought to be one of many mice overrunning their school. They also discussed the harm rodents do to crops and food supplies and the rapidity with which they multiply.'"

There was a murmur of disapproval from

the class as Miss K read on. " 'When informed
of the mouse plague at the monthly meeting
of the school board Friday evening, Superintendent Clyde R. Crossman promised a full

investigation of conditions at Sneed.'"

The class sat in outraged silence. Ralph was aghast. One tiny mouse an invader overrunning the whole school all by himself?

Suddenly everyone had something to say. "Our exhibit wasn't like that at all." "We were having fun, and she made our school sound terrible." "Poor little Ralph didn't invade us. Ryan brought him to school." "She made our school sound dirty, and Mr. Costa works hard." "She was mean not to put our picture in the paper." "She stayed about two minutes and didn't understand what we were doing."

Gordon felt he was to blame for the story. "I didn't mean to get Ralph investigated," he said. "I just wrote facts I found in library books. I didn't mean that Ralph personally ran around harming crops."

Just how am I going to be investigated? Ralph was beginning to wonder.

Brad was pleased that someone else was in the wrong. "I think that reporter is a rat fink," was his contribution to the discussion.

Miss K asked if he couldn't find a better way of expressing himself.

After a moment, he said, "I think that reporter just said what she wanted to say and didn't care about us."

One boy said, "My father says bad news sells more papers than good news."

Everyone agreed that the reporter's saying bad things about their school in order to sell more copies of the *Cucaracha Voice* was mean, unfair, and just plain sneaky. They did good things at their school, and she should have said so.

Melissa said, "I think we should all write letters to the paper and say the story wasn't true and that there is, or was, only one mouse here."

"A splendid idea, Melissa," said Miss K,

always eager for a new project. "We can write letters for our Language Arts class. However, I think we should be careful that *we* tell the truth."

Of course, Room 5 would tell the truth. Room 5 always told the truth, except when they fibbed a little.

Miss K continued. "Can we be sure that Ralph was the only mouse in school? Our principal told me that this morning, after reading the article in last night's *Voice*, the cafeteria workers reported a hole in a bag of sugar and tail tracings in the spilled sugar. The fourth-grade teacher reported that seeds had disappeared from the mosaics her class had made, the librarian said the shredded material from the bags that books are mailed in has been scattered on the carpet, and the first-grade teacher said she found tooth marks in a jar of paste."

This information silenced the class but left Ralph burdened with guilt. He was just a little mouse trying to get along in the world. He had not meant to cause so much trouble.

Melissa spoke out. "Maybe if there are other mice and we can catch Ralph again, we could find him a girlfriend and have a mouse wedding."

"Oh, yes," said the girls, sighing.

The boys were impolite about the suggestion. So was Ralph.

"We don't know where Ralph is," was Miss K's comment, "and perhaps we should wait to write our letters until after the investigation. After all, there may be more mice in the school."

The disappointed class, who had been planning the angry letters they would write to the newspaper, had to agree.

"But Miss K," said Gloria, "isn't your name Heidi?"

Miss K laughed. "Yes, it is."

"Then how come the reporter called you

Bambi?" asked Gloria.

"She must have confused her book characters," was Miss K's amused answer.

Ralph saw nothing to be amused about. What would the investigation mean? Cats?

An exterminator with traps and poisons? Fumigation with deadly fumes seeping through the halls? That new electronic mouser that made a noise only mice could hear and sent them screaming into the night?

Ralph was sure of only one thing. He had to escape from Irwin J. Sneed Elementary School, and he had to escape soon.

8

RALPH SPEAKS

Ralph was tired of skulking about, hiding in mittens and boots, scrounging glue-flavored seeds from fourth-grade mosaics, and eating sugar, which he had overheard children say rotted teeth. He was nervous about the mouse hunt that was about to begin at Sneed Elementary School, all because he had innocently wanted to leave the inn to save an old man's job.

Ralph felt that he was being blamed for everything that went wrong and that trying to be good was not worthwhile.

Ralph left Melissa's boot, because he did not want Ryan to find him. He slipped behind a row of textbooks on health in a bookcase under the window and sat there, pondering large problems such as the unfairness of life and the shortage of liberty and justice for well-meaning mice.

Ralph longed to return to the inn, but he knew that even if he found a way to get there, he could never face the jeering little relatives. First they would demand to know what had happened to his motorcycle. Then they would tell him it served him right that it was broken, because he had been so selfish.

But I've got to go someplace, Ralph decided. Perhaps he could move into a restaurant in Cucaracha. Now that the snow was melting, there was no longer any danger of being buried. However, his feet might freeze, or he might drown in dirty slush. He was too angry with Ryan to ask for help. What Ralph needed was transportation other, of course, than feet.

Ralph tried to make plans. If he could somehow get hold of the pieces of his motorcycle, and if he could manage to nip off a strand of Miss K's strong hair, perhaps he could tie his motorcycle together again.

While Ralph sat brooding behind the books, he was not forgotten by Room 5, who found the problems of a mouse much more interesting than making sentences out of spelling words.

Hands were raised and questions asked. "But Miss K, don't you think we should try to find Ralph? Somebody might step on him." "Miss K, how are they going to investigate the school for mice?" "Miss K, will they poison Ralph?"

Miss K laid down her chalk and gave up trying to teach.

"Miss K," said Ryan. "I'm sure Ralph is the only mouse here. He could have done all those things by himself."

Ryan's remark gave the class hope for Ralph. "I know what we could do," said Melissa. "We could get him to walk across a stamp pad so he would leave purple foot-prints. That way we could see if he went to the cafeteria and the library and all those places."

Ralph groaned. Purple feet! That Melissa and her bright ideas.

The class was quick to point out that the ink would soon wear off, that Ralph would have to keep running back to the stamp pad, which no mouse would do. Anyway, they would have to find him first.

"Well, class," said Miss K, "I can see that we are not going to get any work done until we find out more about the superintendent's investigation. If you will promise to work quietly on your spelling sentences, I will go ask Mr. Tanner what he plans to do."

The class promised. Of course, they would work quietly. Didn't they always work quietly when the teacher left the room? Ralph climbed to the top of a book to watch.

As soon as Miss K left, Melissa, taking the precaution of leaving the door open, posted herself as a lookout. When the teacher was safely out of sight, everyone began to whisper at once. Wads of paper flew back and forth. Ryan pulled the broken motorcycle out of his pocket and said to Brad, "See what you did?"

By standing on his hind legs on top of a book, Ralph was able to see the remains of his motorcycle. More than Miss K's hair was needed to repair that wreck. His motorcycle was broken in two pieces, the muffler dangled, the spring forks were bent, the handlebars twisted. Ralph felt sick looking at it, sick and angry.

Brad scowled. "Why don't you buy him another? You're a rich kid."

Why should he? thought Ralph. Brad was the one who broke it.

"I'm not a rich kid." Ryan was astonished by Brad's remark.

"Then how come you live in a hotel?" demanded Brad.

"Because my mother works there," said Ryan. "I eat in the kitchen with the maids and waitresses."

"Oh." Obviously Brad had not known this. "Where's your father?"

"I don't know." Ryan was sensitive about this subject. "Someplace, I guess."

"Psst!" hissed Melissa, and scooted back to her seat.

Quiet as mice, thought Ralph, as heads

bent over spelling words.

Miss K was smiling as she walked to the front of the room. The class looked up, waiting for her answer. "Mr. Crossman, the superintendent, telephoned Mr. Tanner this morning to ask about mice at Sneed," she told her class. "Mr. Tanner said he didn't think there was much to worry about, that the reporter got carried away. Mr. Crossman said that was good, because since people voted for Proposition 13 and taxes had been cut, the school district couldn't afford an exterminator. Mr. Tanner told him not to worry, that he would have Mr. Costa set mousetraps overnight to see what happened. Mr. Crossman said there was enough money in the budget for five mousetraps."

Traps, thought Ralph. What a joke.

"Was *that* the investigation?" someone asked. "One phone call?"

Miss K laughed. "That was the investigation."

Even though the class was concerned for Ralph's safety, everyone felt let down. They had expected some excitement. A team of men in white uniforms perhaps, and the school closed for several days.

"If Mr. Costa doesn't catch any mice, do we get to write our letters to the *Cucaracha Voice*?" asked Gloria.

"That's right," agreed Miss K.

"But what if Mr. Costa catches Ralph?" someone asked. Others voiced the same worry.

Ralph was insulted. Hadn't he proved his intelligence by finding a new way to run a maze? He knew all about traps. As soon as he was old enough to leave the nest, his mother had taken him to see a baited trap in the hotel kitchen and had explained its evils one by one.

"We'll just have to take that chance,"

said Miss K. "Now please settle down and finish those spelling sentences."

Spelling sentences were all Room 5 did manage that morning. At lunchtime, some of the girls began to call, "Ralphie, where are you, Ralphie?" as they gathered up their lunch boxes.

Ralphie! Ralph would never answer to such a silly name. He noticed Brad was the last to leave, as if he were not eager to join the others for lunch.

Suddenly Ralph's anger boiled over. He did not care if Brad looked lonely. He did not care if Brad found out he could talk. He was going to take matters into his own paws and tell that boy a thing or two.

Ralph leaped lightly from the top of the book, dashed across the floor, and sprang up on Brad's jeans. Desperately he clung by his toenails as Brad walked out of the room and slowly down the hall.

Miss K locked the door of her room and

caught up with Brad, put her arm around his shoulders, and said, "Is there something I can do to help?"

"I'm OK," was all Brad said.

"If I can do anything, please let me know." Miss K released Brad and went on down the hall.

Neither had noticed the mouse clinging to Brad's jeans. Ralph ran up Brad's leg onto the front of his T-shirt.

Finally Brad must have felt Ralph's toenails, for he looked down.

"You—you thug!" said Ralph. "You broke my motorcycle, my only way of getting out of this place. I'm too little to wade through slush, and anyway walking isn't as much fun as riding my motorcycle, especially through puddles."

Brad stared at Ralph. "You can talk," he said, as if he didn't believe it.

"Of course, I can talk," said Ralph. "Not

many people can understand me, but I can talk."

"How come I understand you?" asked Brad.

"You're the type. You're lonesome, and you're interested in cars and motorcycles.

That's the sort of person who understands me." Brad seemed to be thinking this answer over as Ralph continued, "How come you're lonesome? You're not a new boy in school like Ryan."

"None of your business," said Brad. Then, realizing he had admitted more than he intended, he contradicted himself. "I'm not lonesome."

"Aw, come on," coaxed Ralph, who by now was genuinely curious. "You can tell me."

Brad was stubbornly silent.

"I'm just a little mouse, you know," Ralph reminded him.

"Well, I live with my father and Arfy, my dog. My folks got divorced, and my mom doesn't live with us anymore. It's lonesome without her," confessed Brad.

"Oh, too bad." Ralph was sympathetic. His own mother nagged him, but he missed her right now. "Ryan's lonesome too, because he's new here," Ralph told Brad. "You two should get together."

Suddenly Brad laughed, the first time Ralph had ever heard him laugh. "I don't believe this," he said. "A *mouse* telling me what to do."

Ralph's feelings were hurt. "Don't believe it then," he said, remembering his motorcycle.

"Aw, don't be mad." Brad was sorry he had hurt Ralph's feelings. "Let's be friends."

"Why should we?" asked Ralph in his coldest squeak. "You wanted to make the maze too hard; you pushed my friend and broke my motorcycle. Why should we be friends?"

"Because—" began Brad, and then he stopped. "Look. I didn't know Ryan had a motorcycle in his pocket or you either. I thought he was a rich—Oh, never mind what I thought. Was that really your motor-cycle?"

"Yes, it was." Ralph spoke in his crossest voice. "A boy gave it to me."

"Wow!" breathed Brad. "A mouse with a motorcycle! Can you ride it?"

"Not when it's broken," said Ralph. "Now put me down and go eat your lunch. I need a little rest. Mice are supposed to be nocturnal, you know, and I need my sleep in the daytime."

"Miss K locked the door," Brad reminded him, "and you shouldn't be running around the halls where you can get stepped on."

"No problem. I can go under the door," said Ralph.

"Will you talk to me again?" asked Brad, as he used the hand not in the sling to set Ralph on the floor.

"Maybe, maybe not," answered Ralph. "It all depends." With that noncommittal reply, he flattened himself and slipped under the door into the empty classroom. Inside, he entered what had become his home away from home, Melissa's boot. He felt that he had only dozed off when Ryan's hand closed around him.

"Gotcha!" said Ryan.

"Put me down," snarled Ralph, needing his rest.

"Brad was right," said Ryan. "I didn't think you would come back, but he said he found you and you talked to him."

The class began to return and to crowd around Ryan. "You found him!" they said. "Miss K, Ralph's safe!" "Where will we keep him?" "We can't let him get caught in a trap."

"Traps," snapped Ralph. "Do you think I'm stupid?" Only Ryan and Brad understood him.

"Let's put him in the fishbowl for the

time being," said Miss K.

"Oh, no," groaned Ralph. "Not again."

"I think Ralph likes more privacy," said Ryan.

"There's that old mitten that's been lying around," said Melissa. "He could have it to sleep in."

In spite of Ralph's struggles, he found himself once again in the fishbowl, this time with the old mitten. Furious with Ryan for not managing to save him from this indignity, he crawled into the thumb, where he thought mean thoughts about everyone in Room 5.

Just before the last bell rang, Ryan set a bottle cap full of water in the fishbowl along with the corner of a Granola bar Miss K had given him. "Now take it easy," he whispered. "You stay where you're safe tonight, and tomorrow we'll get you out of here. I promise."

Ralph refused to come out of the mitten

thumb to answer. Later, when Mr. Costa came in to sweep, he listened to the radio sing a mournful song about a lonely truck driver in jail who longed for his eighteen-wheel rig and the open highway. And all I want is two wheels, thought sad and lonely Ralph.

9
THE SURPRISE

The next morning Mr. Tanner reported to Miss K and Miss K reported to her class that no mice had been caught in Mr. Costa's traps.

"Yeay!" cheered Room 5.

I told you so, said Ralph from the mitten thumb, but no one heard him.

Miss K wrote the proper form of a business letter instead of a friendly letter on the blackboard, because the class was not planning to write friendly letters to the *Cucaracha Voice*. The class set to work, writing to the editor, explaining that the story he published about the mouse exhibit was not true. If someone had trouble spelling a word, that person asked Miss K about it. She then wrote the word on the blackboard in case someone else wanted to use it. *Outrageous* and *ridiculous* were the first words she wrote. She told Brad, "Yes, *blockhead* is one word, but can't you find a better way of expressing yourself?" Miss K promised personally to deliver the letters to the paper during lunch period.

No matter how many people spoke to him that day, Ralph refused to come out of the mitten thumb, which fortunately already had an excellent peephole. He noticed Brad, who still had his arm in a sling, hand a note to Miss K, who handed it back to him with a nod and a big smile. He saw Ryan pass a note to Brad and Brad pass a note back. Quite a busy bunch, thought Ralph. He was bored and much too warm, but he refused to give anyone the satisfaction of seeing him in his glass prison.

When the long, miserable day ended, Ralph found himself being pulled out of the mitten by Ryan. "Come on, fellow, you're going back to the inn," he said.

"And face all my relatives without my motorcycle," squeaked Ralph. "No, thank you."

"Relax. You can't live at school forever," said Ryan through his teeth, as he tried not to move his lips. "Trust me. Everything is going to be all right. You'll see."

Because Ryan kept his hand closed around him, Ralph had no choice. He had to trust Ryan unless he bit him instead. He decided against doing so, because Miss K said hurting people did not solve anything.

Ryan shoved Ralph into his parka pocket and closed the zipper all the way. Even so, Ralph was aware that something unusual was happening. Brad got on the school bus with Ryan after saying to the driver, "Here's my note from home." The two boys sat together.

"Have you got it?" asked Ryan.

"Yep," answered Brad. "Right here in my pocket."

Got what? Ralph wondered. The remains of my motorcycle?

"I've always wanted to ride on a school bus," said Brad.

"And I've always wanted to ride on a tow truck," said Ryan.

"That's easy," said Brad. "My dad will give you a ride. He gets lots of calls up your way when the roads are icy, and he pulls a lot of cars out of snowbanks. Business is good this time of year."

"I'll ask the cook if you can stay to dinner," said Ryan.

"Wow! Dinner in a hotel." Brad was
impressed.

"We'll have to eat in the kitchen," Ryan

explained, "and since the hotel's got a microwave oven, sometimes the plates are hot and the food isn't."

"That's OK," said Brad. "My dad cooks mostly hamburgers and opens cans of beans." Then, lest Ryan think him disloyal to his father, he added, "My dad makes good hamburgers, and on Sunday he cooks a steak. Sometimes if he's really busy, I get my own supper. Then I have hot dogs."

"You mean you stay alone?" asked Ryan.

"I have Arfy with me," said Brad.

"I wish I could get to stay alone with a dog," said Ryan. "I get tired of hearing the waitresses tell the cook that the guests are complaining because the food isn't hot enough."

Ralph resented being imprisoned by a zipper, and the conversation was boring because it was not about him. He thought about biting his way out, but he did not like the taste of nylon. Besides, a school bus was not a good place to hide.

When the two boys got off the bus, Ralph heard their feet crunch through the snow. The inn was at a higher altitude than the town of Cucaracha, and the snow lasted longer. Then he heard their feet stamp up the steps, scratch on the doormat, and enter the lobby. The old clock was still managing its familiar slow *tick . . . tock*. To Ralph, it sounded like an old friend.

"Hello there, boys," said Ralph's protector, Matt. "Ryan, I'm glad to see you have a friend." So Matt had not lost his job after all. Then, as Ralph had hoped, the little mice must have moved upstairs, where they would be unable to taunt him about losing his motorcycle.

Feeling more cheerful, Ralph began to jump around in the slippery pocket. "Let me out!" he demanded. Ryan unzipped his pocket and lifted Ralph out but held on to him. How good the lobby looked. A fire still burned in the old stone fireplace, and the grandfather clock and television set were right where they had always been. One thing was different. The lobby was neater than Ralph remembered it. Ashtrays were clean, and old magazines arranged neatly on tables.

The desk clerk ignored the boys, who did not stop to remove their jackets before they knelt in front of the clock. "Do you think it will fit?" Ryan asked Brad.

"We'll see in a second." Brad pulled something out of his pocket.

"Wow! A Laser XL7, just like you said," breathed Ryan, as Brad set a miniature sports car on the floor and pushed it carefully through the highest part of the arch at the bottom of the clock. The car was low enough, if maneuvered by a skillful driver, to slip through. "See that, Ralph?"

Ralph had seen, all right. The sleek, mouse-sized car with wire-spoked wheels and knock-off hubcaps was painted silvery gray, the right color for whizzing unnoticed through shadows. The broad thick tires would stand up to the rough surface of carpets and make a wide splash through puddles. The doors did not open, but the windows were big enough for a nimble mouse to climb through, and, after all, racing-car drivers did not open their doors. Ralph was squeakless at the sight of such a beautiful sports car. Why, with a car like that, he would no longer have to hang onto his tail to keep it from tangling in the spokes. He could just hop in and take off.

"Come on. Let's see you drive it." Ryan set Ralph down beside the little Laser XL7.

Could he drive it! He'd show them. Ralph slipped through the window into a bucket seat, made sure his tail was safely inside, grasped the wheel, took a deep breath, and went *pb-pb-b-b*. The car did not move.

Some noisy skiers came in from outdoors but paid no attention to the kneeling boys as they crossed the lobby. The boys crouched behind the couch until they had gone.

"Silly," said Ryan. "That's your old motorcycle noise. You've got to make a sports car noise to make a sports car move."

"Stupid of me," admitted Ralph, who had been too excited to think straight. He took another deep breath, made his voice as low as a squeaky voice could go, and went *vroom-vroom*. The Laser began to roll across the floor. Ralph was driving! He was actually driving this beautiful sports car. He drove it straight into the leg of a couch, where it stopped. Ralph vroomed again. The car did not budge.

Matt, who had joined the boys to watch,

asked, "How's the little fellow going to back up?" Silence. No one had thought of this problem.

Ryan's mother stepped out of the elevator. "Hello, Ryan," she said with a smile. "Is this your new friend?"

"Yes, this is Brad," answered Ryan, with

his hand on the Laser XL7 so his mother would not see Ralph.

"Hi." Brad was unexpectedly shy.

"I'm glad you could come home with Ryan," said Mrs. Bramble. "What are you boys doing?"

"Playing with a little car," said Ryan.

"Play quietly," said Mrs. Bramble, "and if the manager appears, you'd better go out to our cottage. Or perhaps you could show Brad around. He might like to see the kitchen." With that advice, she went off to make sure the maids had cleaned the ground-floor bedrooms properly.

Brad sat back on his heels. "Your mom sure is nice," he said.

"Yes," agreed Ryan, his thoughts on Ralph's problems.

Vroom-vroom-vroom. Ralph made a noise like a racing motor. The car did not move.

"What we need is your dad's tow truck," remarked Ryan. Ralph found the boys' laughter most annoying.

"I know," said Brad. "If going *vroom* makes the car go forward, maybe saying *vroom* backwards would make it back up. *Moorv.*"

"*Moorv.*" Ryan tried out the sound. "It's hard to say, but if it works, that's OK.

Backing a car is slower than going forward. Try it, Ralph."

"Moorv." The car inched away from the leg of the couch. *"Moorv."* The car was free. *"Vroom."* Ralph drove off in a wide circle and returned to his friends. "Do I get to keep it?" he asked.

"It's all yours," said Brad. "To make up for your broken motorcycle."

"Don't you need it?" asked Ralph, unable to believe that anyone would give away such a car.

"Not anymore," Brad told him. "Not since I have a BMX."

Ralph was speechless with joy. He ran his paw lovingly over the dashboard of his very own car.

"Wait till your relatives see you riding around in a Laser XL7," remarked Matt.

Ralph leaned out the driver's window. "What do you mean?" he asked. "I thought they all moved back upstairs."

"Most of them did," said Matt, "but a few of your outdoor relatives still hang around, hoping you'll bring the motorcycle back."

Just my luck, thought Ralph. That rowdy bunch.

There was the sound of someone stamping snow off boots at the entrance of the inn. Matt hastily returned to his chair by the front door while Ralph quickly and skillfully drove his car under the clock. The boots turned out to belong not to a guest but to a man delivering the *Cucaracha Voice*. He shoved the papers into a rack and hurried out.

Matt removed a copy of the newspaper, put on his spectacles, and read the headlines. Then something at the bottom of the front page caught his eye. "Say, do you boys know a Miss Heidi Kuckenbacker down at Sneed?" he asked.

"Yes, she's our teacher." The two boys

rushed over to Matt to see what the paper said about Miss K. Ralph climbed out of his car. He found that bits of his old nest still remained under the clock. With a shred of Kleenex, he began with loving care to polish away the boys' fingerprints. As he polished, he listened while Matt read aloud from the *Voice*.

"'Retraction,' it says here above this picture," said Matt.

"What's *retraction*?" asked Brad.

"It means they take back something they said," explained Matt.

"They should," said Brad.

"Hey, look," said Ryan. "There's the picture of our class. What else does it say?"

Matt read, "'The editors of the *Cucaracha Voice* regret a misleading story published in Saturday's edition concerning Miss Heidi Kuckenbacker's class at Irwin J. Sneed Elementary School.'"

Ralph stopped polishing. Maybe the paper would say something about him.

Matt continued. "'After thorough investigation, Superintendent Clyde R. Crossman has cleared Sneed of charges of mouse infestation. Miss Kuckenbacker's pupils have informed the editor that the mouse exhibited in her classroom was not captured as reported but was instead a pet of Ryan Bramble, a member of the class.'"

Ralph was insulted. He was no one's pet, not Ryan's, not anyone's.

"Hey, Ryan, you got your name in the paper!" Brad was excited for his friend.

"Wait, there's more," said Matt. "'Miss Kuckenbacker reports that she and her class learned much from having a mouse in the classroom.'"

How about that! thought Ralph. I guess I taught them a thing or two.

Matt read on. "'The editors regret any embarrassment caused Room 5 by the misleading article about their activities.'"

"Well, that's better," said Brad.

"Sounds as if maybe that editor is having a little fun," remarked Matt.

"No, he isn't." Ryan was serious.

"We really did write to the paper," said Brad, "and the superintendent really did investigate mice at our school, sort of."

"I guess we took care of that editor," said Ryan. "Come on, Brad, let's go see if the cook will give us something to eat."

Ralph watched the boys leave before he carefully polished every millimeter of his beautiful new car. Then he pushed his nest together for a nap while waiting for night to come. His day had been exciting, exhausting, and satisfying. Because of him, two boys had become friends. Ralph felt that he had done a good deed in a troubled world.

Ralph awoke much later when the clock began to grind and groan and slowly, as if in pain, strike eleven, the safe hour for mice to appear. Ralph was enjoying a good stretch when he saw five of his relatives peering in at him.

"He's back!" said one.

"And he's got a car," said another.

"A sports car," said a third.

Instantly there was clamor and confusion. "Give me a ride!" "Me first!" "Stop shoving!" "I should be first because I'm oldest." "Get off my foot."

Instead of getting excited and angry, Ralph stood calmly beside his car and looked at his relatives without speaking. Gradually the mice grew quiet.

"That's better," said Ralph. "I can't hear anyone if you all speak at once." The mice were silent, listening, the way Room 5 had grown quiet and listened to Miss K.

"Look, class—I mean, fellows," said Ralph, "if you get in line, you can take turns. That way you can each have a ride."

"Good idea," murmured the mice, who had never before thought of such a thing.

Ralph was pleased with himself for putting his education to use. He climbed into his car and drove it out from under the clock. "My oldest cousin first," he directed. His relative climbed into the passenger's seat and pulled his tail in after him. "That's the way," said Ralph with approval. "Now take a deep breath, and we'll both go *vroom*." Together the cousins vroomed around the lobby, down the long hall and back, faster than Ralph could have driven alone.

"Next," Ralph said, when he had returned his passenger. "And by the way," he said to his relatives, as his next cousin in line climbed into the car, "in school human beings learn things by grades. So older human children learn harder things than younger human children."

The mice caught on at once. "Riding in sports cars is for older mice," one cousin said. "It's too dangerous for little mice."

"We won't even tell our little relatives about it," said another.

"We can't have them messing up the lobby," said a third.

"We'll keep it a secret," said a fourth.

"Good thinking," complimented Ralph. As he and his cousins sped down the hall, Ralph was happy. He felt proud because he had helped Miss K educate her class.

But he was humble enough to admit that he had learned from the children too, even though he never did find out where Miss Heidi Kuckenbacker kept her toothpaste. He guessed it really didn't matter.

EPILOGUE

When Brad's father came to the Mountain View Inn in his tow truck to take Brad home, he met Ryan's mother. Six months later they were married, and Ryan and Brad became brothers. They all lived in a house in Cucaracha, California. Ryan was pleased to have a father, and Brad was happy to have a mother. Most of the time the boys were glad to be brothers.

And Ralph? The boys decided that the dog Arfy might take an interest in a mouse for the wrong reason. Ralph remained behind at the inn, where he rides around every night in his sports car, generously giving rides to his relatives and enjoying their company now that they have benefited from his education. He is strict about one thing, however. Ralph is the only mouse who sits in the driver's seat of the Laser XL7.

ALAN MCLWAIN

BEVERLY CLEARY is one of America's most beloved authors. As a child, she struggled with reading and writing. But by third grade, after spending much time in her public library in Portland, Oregon, she found her skills had greatly improved. Before long, her school librarian was saying that she should write children's books when she grew up.

Instead she became a librarian. When a young boy asked her, "Where are the books about kids like us?" she remembered her teacher's encouragement and was inspired to write the books she'd longed to read but couldn't find when she was younger. She based her funny stories on her own neighborhood experiences and the sort of children she knew. And so, the Klickitat Street gang was born!

Mrs. Cleary's books have earned her many prestigious awards, including the American Library Association's Laura Ingalls Wilder Award, presented to her in recognition of her lasting contribution to children's literature. *Dear Mr. Henshaw* won the Newbery Medal, and *Ramona Quimby, Age 8* and *Ramona and Her Father* have been named Newbery Honor Books. Her characters, including Beezus and Ramona Quimby, Henry Huggins, and Ralph, the motorcycle-riding mouse, have delighted children for generations.

Get to know all the beloved characters
in The World of Beverly Cleary at
WWW.BEVERLYCLEARY.COM